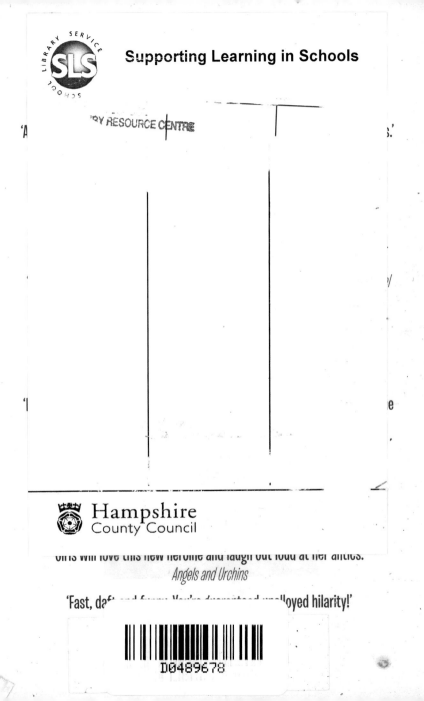

Supporting Learning in Schools

SLS
SCHOOL LIBRARY SERVICE

'A   s.'

'   e

Hampshire
County Council

Girls will love this new heroine and laugh out loud at her antics.
Angels and Urchins

'Fast, daft and funny. You're guaranteed unalloyed hilarity!'

To Rob, with love

EGMONT
We bring stories to life

Ellie May is Totally Happy to
Share her Place in the Spotlight
First published in paperback in Great Britain
2013 by Jelly Pie, an imprint of
Egmont UK Limited
The Yellow Building, 1 Nicholas Road
London W11 4AN

Text copyright © 2013 Marianne Levy
Illustrations copyright © 2013 Ali Pye

The moral rights of the author and illustrator
have been asserted

ISBN 978 1 4052 6030 5

1 3 5 7 9 10 8 6 4 2

www.egmont.co.uk

A CIP catalogue record for this title is
available from the British Library

49952/1

Printed and bound in Great Britain by the
CPI Group (UK) Ltd, Croydon, CR0 4YY

EGMONT

ELLIE MAY

is Totally Happy to Share her Place in the Spotlight

Marianne Levy

EGMONT

Contents

Chapter One

Ellie May is Totally Happy to Share her Place in the Spotlight

'I am very excited about Cassie Craven's party,' said Ellie May, 'because it is a party, and I really like parties. And I really like Cassie, or at least, I'm sure I would if I got to know her a bit better. Yes, I definitely and completely want to go to her party except that I don't really want to go at all.'

'Why not?' asked Jeffrey.

'Because,' said Ellie May, 'everyone will be all, "Cassie, you're amazing!" and, "Cassie, you're so pretty!"'

'That's because it's a party to celebrate the launch of her new film *Pretty Amazing*,' said Jeffrey.

'Exactly,' said Ellie May, twisting a strand of her red hair round her finger. 'Everyone will be busy with her and no one will want to talk to me.'

'You have to get used to not being the centre of attention,' said Jeffrey. 'Life can't always be all about you.'

'Why not?' asked Ellie May. 'I'm much more famous than Cassie. In some countries. And I'm not saying that I need to be the centre of attention *all the time*, Jeffrey. But I do need to be the centre of attention for at least some of the time, because I'm incredibly famous. Otherwise people might forget about me and then I won't be so famous any more. Which would be bad because no one would come and see my films. I like my films, Jeffrey. They're all about me and they're really good. I wish we were at home now. Then we could watch one of them.'

Ellie May was an incredibly famous film star. You probably remember her from the smash hits

Ocean Deep, Give Us a Wave and *Help! There's a Shark in My Paddling Pool!*

At that moment, she was standing outside a hotel in Los Angeles with her chaperone, Jeffrey. On her head, she wore a blue glittery hat. On her feet, blue glittery shoes. Her dress was green and glittery. And her handbag was yellow, but not glittery. Ellie May knew that it was important not to overdo it on the glitter.

'Your films aren't *all* about you,' said Jeffrey crossly. 'You star in them, but there are other people in them as well. And then there's the director and the writer and the sound man and the cameraman and –'

'I know, I know,' said Ellie May. 'There are lots of other people doing lots of other things. I'm just saying that I'm the important one. That's all. Shall we go in?'

'Wait,' said Jeffrey. 'I don't like all this "me me me". I want you to prove that you don't need to be the centre of attention all the time. No signing autographs, no posing for photos. Go in there and be normal. Be nice!'

5

'I can be nice!' said Ellie May. 'And I can definitely be normal. Pass me my cardigan, please, Jeffrey? And my back-up cardigan? Thank you. See you later.' And with that, Ellie May ruffled her hair, smoothed her dress, applied a bit of lipgloss, adjusted the strap of her shoe, checked her blusher, applied a bit more lipgloss and went inside.

What a party it was! The ceiling twinkled with pink fairy lights. Music pounded from pink speakers. Waiters in pink suits held pink trays of pink lemonade. There were pink cakes and pink biscuits and pink bowls of pink sweets. There were even bright-pink crisps, although no one was eating them, for some reason.

And everywhere, there were famous people. There were famous singers and dancers and actors and a dog that had got famous after it had fallen over on the internet. They were all looking at Cassie Craven and saying things like,

'What a fantastic film, Cassie! Are you excited?'

and,

'Are you excited, Cassie? What a fantastic film!'

Ellie May marched right into the middle of the room.

'I'm in a film too,' she said, to no one in particular. 'It starts shooting tomorrow.'

No one in particular didn't seem to be listening.

'It's called *Ugly Duckling*,' continued Ellie May. 'I bet you want to hear all about it.'

Ellie May waited, in case anyone wanted to hear all about *Ugly Duckling*.

Then she did a bit of a twirl.

Then she took a drink from one of the waiters.

Then she did a bit of a dance.

Then she had a couple of sips of her drink.

Then she just stood for a bit.

Then she slowly slunk to one side and sat down in a pink chair.

Meanwhile, Cassie Craven smiled and nodded, as if she was the only person in the whole room that anyone wanted to talk to, which, thought Ellie May sadly, she quite probably was. If this was being normal then being normal was rubbish.

She felt Jeffrey touch her elbow.

'Want to go home?' he whispered.

Ellie May nodded. 'But I ought to stay a tiny bit longer,' she said. 'I haven't said hi to Cassie yet.

Or had any cake. Cassie probably got those little pink cakes in especially for me, which is silly, because she should know that my favourite type is fudge. But even so, I'd better have one before I go. Or maybe two. If I'm being polite.'

'I'll get you some,' said Jeffrey. 'Stay here.'

Ellie May stayed, and sighed. She'd eat her cakes and say goodbye to Cassie. Or maybe she could just wave at her? Or, not wave, and eat the cakes in the car on the way home?

Then, Ellie May saw a girl watching her. A girl about the same age as Ellie May, with wide blue eyes the exact colour of a swimming pool, and long red hair not the exact colour of a swimming pool. Her cheeks were pale and perfect, and her mouth was like a little pink rose.

'Aren't you . . . Ellie May?' asked the girl, in a voice that reminded Ellie May of candyfloss and cream buns. 'You're a film star!'

'An incredibly famous film star, that's right, yes,' said Ellie May. 'And – I recognise you, don't I? You're Fleur! The model! I see you in magazines all the time! Oooh, it's so nice to talk to someone who understands what it's like to be famous. Do people stop you in the street and ask for your autograph?'

'Sometimes,' said Fleur.

'And do they get you to pose for pictures with them?'

'Lots,' said Fleur.

'And do they make T-shirts and have your face printed on them and then outline you with massive sparkly hearts and never take them off, not even when they go to bed or have a bath or go on holiday?' asked Ellie May.

'Um, no, I don't think so,' said Fleur.

'No, they don't for me either,' said Ellie May wistfully. 'But I keep hoping that one day they will.'

'I've always wanted to know,' said Fleur, 'did you do all the juggling in *Juggling Jenny*?'

'Yes! They even gave me lessons,' said Ellie May.

'And for *Karate Kate* did they teach you karate?' asked Fleur.

'They did,' said Ellie May.

'Yay!' said Fleur. 'And when you were in *Headless Helen* did you have to learn how to make your head fall off?'

'No, it was all special effects,' said Ellie May.

14

'That's a shame,' said Fleur. 'It would be fun to be able to take your own head off.'

'Listen!' exclaimed Ellie May. 'They're playing the music from *Dancing Daisy*!'

'Oh!' said Fleur. 'But . . . no. Nothing.'

'What?' asked Ellie May.

'D-Do you think you could teach me the Daisy Dance?' asked Fleur shyly.

'I totally could!' cried Ellie May. 'Come on!' Then, grabbing Fleur by her lovely little hand, Ellie May whirled off towards the dance floor, sending a nearby woman's drink flying into the air like a fizzy comet.

'Ooops!' laughed the woman. She was tall

and angular, like a cross between

a coat hanger, a lamp post

and a woman.

'Sorry about that,' said Jeffrey,

returning with a plateful of cakes.

'I'm Jeffrey, Ellie May's chaperone.

She's being a bit silly this evening,

isn't she? Let me get you another.'

'Thanking you,' said the woman. 'I'll have a wheatgrass juice and soda, please.'

'Gosh,' said Jeffrey. 'I've never heard of that before.'

'You should try it,' said the woman, 'if you want to detox. Go on, have a taste.'

'Do I want to detox?' Jeffrey pondered.

'Oh, you absolutely do,' said the woman. 'Detoxing's brill, Phil.'

'Um, no, actually, it's Jeffrey . . .' began Jeffrey, sipping the drink. 'My word, that's extraordinary! Sorry, what did you say your name was?'

'Penelope,' said the woman, grabbing Jeffrey's

hand and shaking it. 'And newsflash, Jeffrey, I'm a chaperone too!'

'And forward and back and one, two, three, kick!' cried Ellie May. 'Oh, you nearly had it that time, Fleur! If you hadn't hit yourself in the face right at the end there, it would have been perfect.'

'Yay!' cried Fleur.

'I love how we're the same height and we've got the same colour hair,' said Ellie May, leading her new friend off the dance floor. 'I bet I could be a model. What's it like? It must be amazingly amazing.'

'It's nice,' said Fleur. 'But it can't be as fun as being in films. All I ever do is wear fashionable clothes. But you get to act and dance and fly –'

'Fly?' repeated Ellie May.

'In *Wendy's Wings*,' explained Fleur.

'No, that was just special effects again,' said Ellie May. 'And anyway, the point is, *you* get to dress up and have your hair done and go on the catwalk with actual cats.'

'There aren't cats on the catwalk,' said Fleur.

'Don't be silly,' said Ellie May. 'Of course there are! Otherwise why would it be called that?'

'I hadn't ever thought about it,' said Fleur.

'I suppose the cats must be invisible.'

'Can you get invisible cats?' wondered
Ellie May. 'Isn't it impossible for things to be
invisible, really?'

'You went invisible at the end of *Judith The Obscure*,' said Fleur.

'Yes, but that was spe–' Fleur's smile began to droop. 'Yes,' said Ellie May. 'Yes, I suppose I did go invisible.' She grinned at her new friend. It would be a shame when the party finished and they had to go home.

'I bet you really love being a film star,' said Fleur.

'I do,' said Ellie May. 'And I bet you really love being a model.'

'I do, I suppose,' said Fleur, her head hanging like a wilted daffodil. 'But what I really want, more than anything in the world, is –'

'A puppy?' asked Ellie May.

'It's –'

'More shoes!' cried Ellie May.

'What I really want,' said Fleur softly, 'is to be in a film. Like you.'

'Well, why don't you?' asked Ellie May.

'Everyone thinks that models can't act,' explained Fleur, her perfect little forehead creasing into a perfect little frown. 'Everyone thinks we're stupid, that the only reason we exist is to sit around looking pretty. Like pot plants. Or books.'

'I was in a film about a pot plant once,' said Ellie May. 'It was called *A New Leaf* and it had an enchanted watering can.'

'Oh, Ellie May, I'd do anything to be in a film,' said Fleur. 'Anything.'

'You want this even more than you want a puppy, don't you?' said Ellie May.

'I do,' said Fleur.

'Wow,' said Ellie May. 'Even more than a puppy.'

'I don't actually want a pup–' began Fleur.

'I've got an idea,' said Ellie May. 'How would you like a part in *Ugly Duckling*? I can't promise anything, and even if I managed to get it, you would probably only be in one or two scenes, but still?'

Fleur's eyes sparkled as if, high above the swimming pool, the sun had come out.

'Really?' she whispered.

'Of course!' said Ellie May.

'Ellie May,' called Jeffrey, 'the party's finishing soon. Do you still want these cakes?'

'Coming, Jeffrey!' cried Ellie May.

'I'd better go too,' said Fleur.

'It was stunningly fantastic to meet you, Fleur,' said Ellie May. 'I'm going to get my people to call your people tomorrow. Or maybe I'll just call you. Yes, that would probably be easier, wouldn't it?'

'You really don't have to,' said Fleur.

'See you very soon,' winked Ellie May.

Ellie May beamed up at her chaperone across a heap of pink cake.

'Sorry I left you for so long, Jeffrey,' she said. 'I know you wanted to go home.'

'Actually, I've been looking forward to this party,' said Jeffrey. 'It's you who didn't want to come. And guess what?'

'What?' asked Ellie May. 'No, don't tell me.

26

I want to see if I can get it. It's . . . something . . . about . . . a puppy? Have you got me a puppy, Jeffrey? Have you?'

'Er, no,' said Jeffrey. 'I got chatting to another chaperone! She was telling me all about this new –'

'Did you see? Did you see?' squawked Ellie May. 'I made a friend like a nice normal person makes friends, just like you told me to!'

'Well done!' said Jeffrey. 'What's she like?'

'She's a model!' said Ellie May. 'She's really sweet and she wants to be in a film so I said I'd see if I could get her a part in *Ugly Duckling*! I can ask tomorrow. It's just like you wanted, Jeffrey!

I'm not thinking about myself at all any more. I'm only thinking about Fleur.'

'Your new friend is *Fleur*?' said Jeffrey. 'Ooh! Did you manage to get her autograph?'

'Why would I want Fleur's autograph?' asked Ellie May.

'Because she's really famous,' said Jeffrey.

'She's quite famous, I suppose,' said Ellie May. 'Anyway. I was just wondering, would you like *my* autograph?'

'Why would I want your autograph?' asked Jeffrey. 'I see you every day.'

'Because I'm incredibly famous,' said Ellie May.

'Much more famous than Fleur. People are staring at me right now! That's how famous I am.'

'People are staring at you because you've got icing all around your mouth,' said Jeffrey. 'And on your nose. And – how did you manage to get it in your *hair*?'

'Oh,' said Ellie May.

'Look,' said Jeffrey. 'Of course you can see if Fleur can have a part in your film. I just wonder whether this is a good idea? I mean, you've never liked sharing the spotlight.'

'I am totally happy to share my place in the spotlight,' said Ellie May. 'Totally and completely and extremely happy. And I'm extra-specially happy to share it with someone as massively amazing as Fleur.'

'Well, so long as we've got that sorted out,' said Jeffrey.

Chapter Two

Ellie May Will Always Remember her First Film

Ellie May loved everything about her first day on a new film. She loved moving into her trailer. She loved meeting the catering crew and telling them all about precisely the sort of cake she wanted to eat, which was fudge, and how much of it they should be baking, which was a lot. Most of all, she loved making friends with the writer, so that she'd definitely get all the best lines.

She banged on the trailer door marked

DO NOT DISTURB

'Knock knock!' she said. 'It's your favourite incredibly famous film star, here to say hello!'

'We're in the middle of a meeting,' shouted the writer. 'Go away.'

'No, no,' cried the director, 'come in, come in!' She glared at the writer. 'That's *Ellie May*! Our star!

If she wants to come in, she comes in.'

'Of course,' said the writer grumpily. 'Just my little joke.'

'Ha!' giggled Ellie May. 'Like you'd ever really want me to go away. That's funny!'

The director raised an eyebrow.

'Ha ha ha,' said the writer. 'Fine. Come in. Go over there and sit quietly. Don't touch anything. Right, as I was saying before we were interrupted, the problem with scene seventeen is . . .'

'What is it, Ellie May?' asked the director. 'How can we help you? You haven't run out of fudge cake or anything, have you? I did tell the catering crew –'

'No, I've got lots of fudge cake, thank you,' said Ellie May. 'Actually, I was just wondering, I met this girl, yesterday, at Cassie Craven's party. She's ever so pretty and really nice. So I just thought I'd see whether you could maybe give her a part in the film, please?'

'Seriously?' said the writer. 'You meet some girl at a party and next thing you're offering her a part in *my* film?'

'Yes!' said Ellie May.

'I'd love to help,' said the director, 'but it's a bit late now. We're about to start shooting. I wish you'd asked me this a week ago.'

Ellie May's face fell. It didn't fall very far, because it was joined to her head, but even so, the director saw, and frowned.

'I'm sorry, Ellie May,' she said. 'You're our star and I only want to make you happy, I really do. But we don't know whether your friend is any good at acting and –'

'Yes we do!' cried Ellie May.

'Ah!' said the director. 'If she can act, then that's a different matter entirely. What might I have seen her in?'

'Um,' said Ellie May. 'She's, er, not been in

any films, exactly . . . but she's an incredible actress.

I saw her in a musical. In London. She played . . .'

Ellie May thought fast, 'a girl . . . who got ill . . . with

this rare disease . . . and she was beautiful . . . and

brave . . . and then her legs fell off.'

'It sounds *stupendous*,' drawled the writer.

'It was!' said Ellie May. 'And she was really brilliant and won awards and everything.'

'Hmm,' said the director. 'An award-winning stage actress, you say. We could always do with a few more of those around. This is rather exciting. Clever old you, Ellie May! Let's have her as one of the nasty girls who's horrible to you, at the start, when you're ugly.' She turned to the writer. 'You could put in an extra scene, couldn't you?'

'I'm busy,' said the writer.

'Busy making *Ugly Duckling* the best film ever!' said the director. 'So that's that. The costume department can put together an outfit for her, but there won't be time to get a trailer delivered. Still, maybe we –'

'She can share with me! She can share with me!' cried Ellie May. 'Hooray! This is amazing! Thank you! I'm so happy! Hooray! Hooray! Hooray!'

'And if you're happy, we're happy,' added the director. She turned to the writer. '*Aren't we*?'

The writer scowled. 'Hooray,' he said.

Back in her own trailer the next morning, Ellie May rummaged about in the fridge. 'We need to get some cucumbers,' she said. 'Models eat cucumbers. I read it in *Giggle* magazine. Let's make a shopping list. Right. Cucumbers. And some fudge cake, that's for me. Do you think Fleur will want any fudge cake? I'd better put some down for her, just in case. Oooh, maybe I'll want cucumbers too? Yes, I probably will, if I see her eating them. So that's:

cucumbers
fudge cake
fudge cake
cucumbers
a puppy

39

'Er, no,' said Jeffrey, reaching over to cross off 'puppy'. 'And if Fleur wants salad then we've got loads of tomatoes.'

'Yuck,' said Ellie May, taking a tomato from the fridge and giving it a suspicious sniff. 'Who has tomatoes these days? I bet Fleur will hate this. It's so red and yucky.'

'Then put it back,' said Jeffrey.

'I will, just as soon as I've finished making sure that I definitely don't like it,' said Ellie May, popping the tomato into her mouth and reaching for another. 'You will be nice to Fleur, won't you?'

'Why wouldn't I be nice to Fleur?' asked

Jeffrey. 'Honestly, Ellie May. It's going to be fine.'

'It's going to be *brilliant*,' corrected Ellie May. 'We can learn our lines together and paint our nails and wear pyjamas and stuff. It'll be like being in a film!'

'You are in a film,' said Jeffrey.

'I mean, like being in a film where I'm friends with another girl,' said Ellie May.

'You are in a film where you're friends with another girl,' said Jeffrey.

'But not till I turn beautiful at the end,' explained Ellie May. 'Till then, no one will be friends with me because I'm the ugly duckling. Oh. We've run out of tomatoes.'

There was a delicate knock, and then another.

'Hello?' said Fleur, peeking round the edge of the trailer door. 'Is this the right place?'

'Fleuuuuuuuur! Come in come in is that bag new where did you get it this is so exciting sorry we haven't got any cucumbers,' said Ellie May.

'Hello, Fleur,' said Jeffrey. 'I'm Ellie May's chaperone. My name's Jeffrey.'

'Hello, Jeffrey,' quivered Fleur.

'It's all right, don't be scared,' said Jeffrey.

'The director said to drop my bags off here and then go over to get fitted for my costume,' said Fleur. 'She did tell me where it is but . . . I think

42

I've forgotten.'

'I'll show you, I'll show you let me show you let me!' cried Ellie May, dragging Fleur back outside. 'So, this is the film set, and there's where the director sits, in the chair with DIRECTOR written on it. And there's my chair, with ELLIE MAY on the back. And on the front. And on the sides, and underneath. I had it made specially.'

'And there's my chair,' said Jeffrey. 'The one with JEFFREY written on it. Once.'

'You've got your own bakery here!' said Fleur. She ran across to the bakery door and gave it a push. 'Oh. It's locked.'

'That's the backdrop,' said Ellie May. 'It isn't real. It's made of a big flat piece of wood with windows and doors and things painted on. Isn't it clever?'

'Yes, very,' said Fleur. 'Oh, there's a sweet shop! Look at those sugar mice!' She scrabbled at the door handle. 'Maybe it's closed. But the sign says "Open".'

'The sweet shop's not real either,' said Ellie May. 'It's another part of the set. The whole street is pretend. Look, see, there's nothing behind it. And that's the costume trailer, over there.'

'Um,' said Fleur.

'What?' asked Jeffrey.

'Well, it's just, I don't know how I'm going to

46

get fitted for my costume,' said Fleur.

'You go in and meet the costume lady –' began Jeffrey.

'But how?' asked Fleur. 'None of the doors will open.'

'The costume trailer *is* real,' said Ellie May. 'You can open the door and go inside. Come on, I'll show you.'

'Bye then,' said Jeffrey. 'And break a leg, Fleur!'

Fleur bit her lip. 'Oh,' she said. 'I didn't think filming would be dangerous.'

Jeffrey's eyes twinkled. 'Well, you never

know,' he said. 'When there are crocodiles . . .'

'Crocodiles?' squeaked Fleur. 'No one said there would be crocodiles!'

'Only a couple,' grinned Jeffrey. 'And I don't suppose they will be *very* hungry . . .'

Fleur's beautiful eyes filled with beautiful tears.

'Hey! I'm only teasing,' cried Jeffrey. 'Of course there aren't any crocodiles! "Break a leg" is a special actors' way of saying good luck! I was just being silly. Come on, give me a smile?'

Fleur smiled a tiny little smile.

'There we are,' said Jeffrey.

Ellie May shot Jeffrey a glare. 'You go and wait by the costume trailer, Fleur,' she said. 'I'll be with you in just a second.'

Fleur trotted away. When she had safely gone, Ellie May put her hands on to her hips. 'Jeffrey,' she said. 'What did I just tell you about being nice to Fleur?'

'I *was* nice to her,' protested Jeffrey.

'You told her she was going to have her leg broken off and eaten by a crocodile,' said Ellie May.

'I was teasing! I didn't think she would believe me!' said Jeffrey. 'What are you looking like that for? Are you all right?'

'I am making my angriest face,' said Ellie May, 'to show how very angry I am. Fleur is my guest and my friend and from now on I want you to be nice to her. And not in a way that makes her think that she is going to be eaten by a crocodile. Goodbye.' And with that, Ellie May stomped off towards the costume trailer.

Jeffrey stood for a moment, then he turned and went back inside. It was nice, sometimes, having the trailer all to himself. He had just sat down on the tomato that Ellie May had thoughtfully left on the sofa, when there was another knock at the door.

'What have you forgotten, Ellie May?' he

called. 'If it's your script, then it must be in the car, because I can't see it anywhere.'

'Hey there!' said a familiar voice, and then into the doorway stepped a woman who looked a bit like a folded-up deckchair, if it was the sort of folded-up deckchair that somehow looked a bit like a woman.

'Penelope!' exclaimed Jeffrey. 'You're –'

'Fleur's chaperone,' beamed Penelope. 'Great to see you again, J-man. Looks like we're going to be trailer buddies. Budge up, I'm coming in!'

Ellie May and Fleur stood on set together, ready to rehearse their scene. Ellie May was grinning, but Fleur was glancing around like a wild animal that had somehow strayed somewhere it shouldn't have, for example a shop or a museum or a film set.

'What's that over there?' she asked.

'That's the camera track,' said Ellie May.
'The cameraman pushes the camera along it.'

'What's that?' Fleur pointed.

'That's the monitor,' said Ellie May. 'It's like
a little television. The director watches the bits we
film on it, to see how good we were.'

'And what's that?' asked Fleur.

'That's the
stuntman,' said Ellie
May. 'He's pretending he's
been hit by an arrow. No, actually,
I think he *has* been hit by an arrow.
It's quite a dangerous job.'

'Ready to rehearse in five!' called the director.

'Your first rehearsal for your first film,' sighed Ellie May. 'You'll never forget it. I'll always remember my first film.'

'What was it?' asked Fleur.

'It was called, um, something something something *Onion*,' said Ellie May. 'I think it was a film about an onion. Or something.'

'I hope I won't forget this,' said Fleur. 'I think I've forgotten my lines already.'

'Didn't you learn them?' asked Ellie May.

'I thought I had. But they keep going out of my head,' confessed Fleur.

54

Ellie May smiled, but behind her smile she was starting to feel a tiny bit worried. Maybe what Fleur had said was right? Maybe models *couldn't* act. Fleur was looking exceptionally pretty; there was no doubt about that. Her hair was shining. Her eyes were shining. Even her teeth were sort of shining! But she also looked small and pale and a little afraid. Ellie May felt a rush of affection for her shiny new friend.

'If I ever get scared, which I don't, obviously, but if I do, I always try to imagine what everyone would look like sitting on the toilet,' said Ellie May. 'Does that help? You sometimes have to imagine

55

quite a lot of toilets, but I am very good at that. Mine are always peach-coloured. I don't know why.'

'OK,' whimpered Fleur. 'My mouth's just gone all dry.'

'Lick your teeth before you start to speak,' said Ellie May.

'I will,' said Fleur. 'Oh, Ellie May, I'm a bit frightened. And not just because of the crocodiles. It's been my dream, my whole life, to be in a film. What if I mess it up?'

'Just try to relax,' said Ellie May, doing her best to smile. 'You're not going to mess it up. I mean, just think how embarrassing it would be!

56

There. Does that help?'

'Right,' said the director. 'Let's go. Chin up, Fleur. There's really nothing to worry about. Now, we won't use real ice cream today, so just pretend you've got one. Ellie May, if you could stand on this spot here? And Fleur, you're over there.'

'I believe in you, Fleur,' said Ellie May.

'Really?' whispered Fleur.

'Of course!' said Ellie May. 'You can do this! Probably!'

'That's perfect,' said the director. 'OK, so here we go with the rehearsal. Quiet everyone. And – action!'

Ellie May leaned up to the ice-cream van window.

'Mint choc chip, please,' she said.

Fleur stalked across the set and pretended to snatch

the cone away.

'But that's mine!' stuttered Ellie May.

'Oh dear, did I push in front of you?' jeered Fleur.

She took a big imaginary bite of the ice cream. 'You're so

plain and boring that I didn't even notice you were here!'

'And . . . cut!' called the director. 'Oh, my goodness!'

'Incredible!' said the sound man.

'Extraordinary,' said the cameraman.

'What a performance!' exclaimed the director.

'Oh, well, really, it wasn't *that* good,' grinned Ellie May.

'No, it was, it was!' said the director.

'Wonderful,' murmured the make-up artist.

'Astonishing,' sighed the stuntman.

'Hooray for Fleur!' cried the director.

'Oh,' said Ellie May.

Chapter Three

Ellie May Can Easily Handle her New Friend's Success

Back in the trailer, Jeffrey watched as Penelope opened an enormous bag and started depositing the contents on the table.

'Goodness,' he said.

'It's always best to bring your own food and

drink, isn't it?' said Penelope. 'You just can't rely on other people to have everything you need.'

'I know!' agreed Jeffrey. 'The catering van once ran out of fudge cake and . . . well. I still can't really talk about it.'

'Or even if they have got everything, it's not usually organic,' said Penelope, lighting a scented candle. 'So, what's the plan, Stan?'

'Stan?' Jeffrey looked around. 'Oh, you mean me. I don't really have a plan, exactly. Just wait till Ellie May gets back, I suppose.'

'Where do your cups live?' asked Penelope. 'Ah, here we are. I'm just going to whip up an energy drink for Fleur. Very simple, a little agave nectar, some soya milk and fresh ginger. *Ta da*!'

'Golly,' said Jeffrey. 'What a treat.'

'A treat?' Penelope grinned. 'Newsflash, J-man. Fleur has them every day. Would Ellie May like one too?'

Jeffrey stared. 'Possibly,' he said. 'I'm not quite sure, to be honest.'

'Oh, sorry, how rude of me coming in and taking over everything!' exclaimed Penelope. 'You'll have your own special recipe, I imagine.'

'Um,' said Jeffrey. 'Yes. I do have my own

special recipe. Definitely. Very special. And I have all the ingredients I need right here. Yes.'

He scanned the kitchen. 'I just mix up, er . . . milk and lemonade and a bit of coffee, a pinch of salt and . . . cornflakes.'

'Cornflakes?' said Penelope, watching Jeffrey shaking a handful over his glass.

Jeffrey considered his creation. 'Maybe it would be better without cornflakes. It does look a bit odd, doesn't it? I'll do another one –'

'We're back,' announced Ellie May, trotting up the trailer steps, through the door, and flopping down on to the sofa.

'How did your rehearsal go?' asked Jeffrey, sliding his energy drink into a cupboard where no one could see it.

'All right, I think,' said Fleur.

'Fleur was great,' said Ellie May flatly. 'I can

totally see why she won all those awards for that musical.'

'What musical?' asked Fleur.

'See, there was nothing to be afraid of!' smiled Jeffrey. 'How about you, Ellie May?'

'My bits were fine,' said Ellie May. 'I suppose. Nobody said anything about them.'

'Ellie May was amazing,' said Fleur. 'And she was really kind. I got scared but she gave me loads of brilliant advice. And then I started acting and I didn't feel nervous at all!'

'See? You're a natural,' said Jeffrey. 'Now, ladies, take a seat and –'

'Hey there, Ellie May, I'm Penelope, Fleur's chaperone,' said Penelope. 'Want an all-natural home-mixed special-recipe energy drink? It's scrummerlicious!'

'Yay!' said Fleur.

'Wow,' said Ellie May, accepting a glass from Penelope's outstretched hand. 'Jeffrey, have you seen this?'

'Yes, I saw it,' muttered Jeffrey.

Ellie May took a sip. 'Yum! Can we start having these? Please please can we pleeease?'

'Of course,' said Jeffrey. 'I didn't know you wanted them. I'm sorry.'

'I absolutely do,' said Ellie May, emptying her glass. 'I can't believe you made that yourself, Penelope. You're incredible! Can I have another one?'

'Well, it's your lucky day,' said Jeffrey, reaching for the cupboard door. 'Surprise!'

'Are you *sure* . . .' began Penelope.

'Is it a puppy?' asked Ellie May.

'No, it's not a puppy,' said Jeffrey. 'It's something even better. *I've* made you an energy drink too. A secret surprise energy drink.' He held out a full glass. 'Scrummerino!'

Ellie May regarded the drink. 'Er,' she said, 'I think I'll stick with Penelope's for now. But thank you, Jeffrey. Yours looks very nice too. In a lumpy sort of a way.'

'It's absolutely delicious,' said Jeffrey. 'See?' He took a big swallow.

'Is it?' said Fleur doubtfully.

'Yes!' Jeffrey tipped back the glass and drank with noisy glugs. 'Lovely. The coffee granules didn't quite dissolve. And the cornflakes have gone a bit soggy. But that only makes it better, really. Gives it an interesting texture. Hic! Are you sure you don't want some? I can easily make more. Hic!'

Ellie May started to giggle.

'Hic!' hiccupped Jeffrey. 'It must have been the

bubbles in the lemonade. Make sure you drink yours a bit more slowly. Hic! Excuse me, Penelope. Hic!'

'I know a way to cure hiccups,' said Ellie May. 'You go to bed and eat ten oranges. No, wait, that's how to cure a cold. And it doesn't actually work.'

'Hic!' said Jeffrey. 'Sorry! Hic!'

'You can drink a glass of water backwards,' said Fleur. 'I've never seen anyone do it, though. What do you think the "backwards" part means? Would you have to drink it hanging upside down?'

'It really doesn't matter,' said Jeffrey. 'I think – hic! – the best thing to do would be to carry on as – hic! – normal and pretend that – hic!

Hic! Hic! Oh dear.'

'Having a fright can cure hiccups, can't it?' said Fleur. 'Boo!'

'BOO! BOO! BOO!' shrieked Ellie May, bouncing up and down like a hyperactive grasshopper.

'Hic!' said Jeffrey. 'Penelope, I promise, we're not normally like this. *Are we*, Ellie May?!'

'That wasn't frightening enough,' said Ellie May. She looked around the trailer. 'Hmm. How about if I throw a cushion at you? Or, a chair?'

'No, don't – hic! Hic! Don't throw a chair at me – hic!' said Jeffrey, edging away backwards.

'That's incredibly dangerous.'

'I *know*,' said Ellie May, following Jeffrey over to the sofa. 'Obviously it's dangerous. That's why it's so frightening.'

'Can we – hic! – change the subject?' pleaded Jeffrey.

'How about if I ask the film crew whether they would set off an explosion?' suggested Ellie May helpfully. 'Or we could get the stuntman to push you out of a helicopter? Ooh! Yes! Let's definitely do that!'

'So, Penelope,' began Jeffrey desperately, 'is this the – hic! – first time you've been on a film set? If you need to know anything, you – hic! – you must ask. Hic! Hic!'

'Now, Jeffrey,' said Penelope, laying a cool hand upon his arm. 'Don't look so ashamed. These things happen to the best of us.'

'Oh – hic! – good,' gasped Jeffrey. 'I'm glad you understand.'

'I understand completely,' said Penelope. 'There's no need to be embarrassed.'

'Thank – hic! – you,' said Jeffrey.

'It's awful when this sort of thing happens,' said Penelope, 'because you feel so out of control. But it's totally natural and can't be helped. No one's laughing at you. I promise.'

'Actually, I am, a bit . . .' said Ellie May.

'So,' said Jeffrey, 'we'll just carry on as – hic! – as though nothing's happening? They'll have to stop eventually. Hic!'

'I need you to stand on your head,' said Penelope.

'On my – hic!'

'Yes, that's right. On your head. It rebalances the body's internal forces. Just tip forward, legs up and – there we are! Can you feel your life force being rebalanced?'

'Er – hic! – maybe?' said Jeffrey. 'All the blood's rushing to my brain, if that's what you mean. Hic!

Can I please get back up again?'

'While you're upside down, you can drink a glass of water backwards,' said Fleur. 'Look, there's

a bit of your brown lumpy stuff left. Open your mouth?'

'Boo!' yelled Ellie May, thwacking at Jeffrey with a cushion. 'Is this helping? BOO! BOOOOO!'

'Oh, dear,' spluttered Jeffrey. 'Please don't, I'll fall . . . this is so embarrassing . . . I don't . . . argh, I've got cornflakes up my nose!

Stop it, Ellie May, I'm going to fall over! Oh dear!

Oh dear! Oh dear! Hic!'

Ellie May walked slowly back to the film set. It was a lovely afternoon. Sunshine glinted off the cameras. The backdrop creaked in the breeze. Tiny fragments of glass flew into the sky like handfuls of glittering gems, closely followed by the stuntman, who was falling through a stained-glass window. It couldn't have been a more glorious day, thought Ellie May, and there really wasn't anything nicer than being an incredibly famous film star.

'Hello,' she said to the cameraman, who was setting up his camera.

'Hello, Ellie May,' said the cameraman. 'I like your friend Fleur. She's good, isn't she?'

'Yes,' said Ellie May.

'You wouldn't think that this was the first time she'd ever acted in a film, would you?' said the cameraman. 'She seems like she's been doing it forever.'

'Does she?' asked Ellie May.

'That scene with the two of you is going to be terrific,' said the sound man, adjusting his microphone. 'When Fleur's acting you just can't look anywhere else!'

'Right,' said Ellie May.

'And she seems nice, doesn't she?' said the cameraman.

'She does!' said the sound man. 'Really nice.'

'I'm nice,' said Ellie May. 'Plus, I'm incredibly famous.'

She frowned, and then shrugged. She was just being silly. Like Jeffrey had said, back at Cassie's party, life really wasn't *all* about her. Maybe it was time someone else enjoyed a little bit of attention? Yes, it definitely probably maybe possibly was.

Ellie May smiled. It was a smile almost as big as a normal smile. No one would ever have known that she was only acting as if she was cheerful. And that, thought Ellie May, was because she was an amazingly good actress. Because she had been an incredibly famous film star for years and years and years. She could easily handle her new friend's success. In fact, it was impossible for anyone to tell that she wasn't perfectly happy.

'Are you all right, Ellie May?' asked the director. 'You look awfully miserable. How can we cheer you up? We can't have our superstar feeling sad.'

'I'm fine,' said Ellie May. 'Really, I am. Don't

worry about me. I'm sure that I'll be all right.'

'Where's your lovely little friend?' said the director. She looked around. 'Fleur? Where've you gone? Come and see Ellie May.'

'Hello, Ellie May!' said Fleur, coming out from behind the backdrop. 'I've just been talking to the stuntman. He's so funny.'

'I know,' said Ellie May.

'He showed me this thing where he gets a sword and swallows it all the way down,' said Fleur.

'Yes, he's done that for me, too,' said Ellie May. 'Lots of times. I'm really bored of it, he does it so often.'

'OK,' said the director. 'This one's a rehearsal for lighting, cameras and sound. Ellie May and Fleur, could you take your places, please?' She looked down at her monitor. 'Wow! Fleur, you have stunningly beautiful skin! You can really see it on the close-up. Hold on, both of you, it'll be just a couple more minutes, I want to change the shot an eeny weeny bit. Gosh, it's warm under these lights, isn't it? Someone give the girls some water!'

'Um, what's my line again?' murmured Fleur. 'Oh, yes, I remember. *"You're so plain and boring."* Plain and boring. Plain and boring.'

Ellie May stood very still as the crew

moved their cameras. It was probably just the heat from the lights, but she felt pink and sweaty and cross. No one had ever called *her* stunningly beautiful.

'Ellie May?'

It was Fleur.

'What?' asked Ellie May.

'My mouth's gone all dry again,' whispered Fleur. 'I've licked my teeth and everything.'

'Then have some water,' snapped Ellie May.

'Of course,' said Fleur meekly. 'Would you like some too? There's fizzy or still.'

'Not long now,' called the director. 'I'm just

watching our last rehearsal. You're a terrific actress, you know, Fleur. So keep shining like the fabulous star that you are!'

Yes, Ellie May realised, the director was right. Fleur was talented and beautiful and sweet. Fleur didn't mind sharing the spotlight. In fact, she was just about perfect. Why couldn't there be *something* wrong with her? Something like . . . something like . . .

And then, Ellie May had an idea.

A terrible, wonderful idea. An idea as tempting and delicious as someone else's fudge cake.

'Actually,' said Ellie May, 'there's a good way to make sure that your mouth doesn't get dry again. Take a bottle of water, the fizzy one, and drink it as fast as you possibly can.'

'Really?' said Fleur.

'Really,' said Ellie May. 'Us actors do it all the time.'

Fleur took an enormous swallow of fizzy water and then another, and another.

'Better?' asked Ellie May.

Fleur gulped and nodded.

'OK, crew, ready for your rehearsal?' called the director. 'And – action!'

Ellie May leaned up to the ice-cream van window. 'Mint choc chip, please,' she said.

Fleur stalked across the set and pretended to snatch the cone away.

'But that's mine!' stuttered Ellie May.

'Oh dear, did I push in front of you?' jeered Fleur. 'You're so plain and boring that – hic!'

'Cut!' called the director. 'Fleur, have you got hiccups?'

'Hic!' hiccupped Fleur, a hot flush spreading across her anguished little face. 'I'm so sorry. Hic!'

'Right, everyone stop,' said the director. 'We'll have to break now. What a pain! We'd only just got started! And you were doing so well, too, Fleur. Still, not to worry, I suppose. Take five, everyone.'

84

Chapter Four

Ellie May is Not a Pea

'Hello, Ellie May, hello, Fleur,' said Jeffrey.

'Hey, kiddos!' cried Penelope. 'How'd it go?'

'It was . . . um . . . all right,' said Ellie May.

'Great,' said Jeffrey. 'And I heard that you've

been working very hard, Fleur. Everyone's been

telling me how wonderful you are . . . Seems that

you're the darling of the film set! Ellie May? Are you growling?'

'No,' said Ellie May. 'That's my tummy. I'm hungry.'

'Then how about a snack?' suggested Penelope. 'Natural yogurt? I make my own, you know. It's got honey and nutmeg in it. *Mm-mm*! Yummity yum!'

'I've made a snack too,' cried Jeffrey. 'It's raw muesli topped with maple syrup and a pinch of cinnamon. And I've mixed you a brand new energy drink. Yummity yum yum yum!'

'You don't need to do all this,' said Ellie May.

'No, I do,' said Jeffrey. 'I've been thinking about what you said, Ellie May. Fleur is your guest and your friend and I really should do everything I can to make her feel at home. And not just her. You, too.'

Ellie May smiled weakly at Fleur. 'My guest,' she murmured. 'My friend.'

'So, what do you want to eat?' asked Penelope. 'Yogurt? Muesli? Some shredded papaya? Or I've whipped up a couple of macrobiotic granola bars, if you'd rather.'

'Actually,' said Ellie May, 'I'm not feeling hungry any more.'

88

'Fleur, you'll have a granola bar?' said Penelope. 'Now, honey-bun, come and sit down here and let me give your shoulders a rub.'

'Thank you, Penelope,' said Fleur.

'Uh, Jeffrey,' said Ellie May, 'what on earth are you doing? Give me back my hairband!'

'I was about to give you a head massage,' said Jeffrey.

'But I don't want a head massage,' said Ellie May.

'Sorry,' said Jeffrey.

'Can I talk to you about something, Jeffrey?' asked Ellie May.

'You absolutely can,' said Jeffrey. 'What is it, sweet pea?'

'Er,' said Ellie May. 'Well. Why are you calling me a pea? I'm not a pea. I'm a May. An Ellie May. *The* Ellie May.'

'Hot towel?' asked Penelope. 'For your pores?'

'Thank you,' said Fleur.

'I can do you a hot towel, if you'd like one, Ellie May!' cried Jeffrey.

'Um, all right, but –' began Ellie May.

'Just a tick!' called Jeffrey.

'Where's the stereo?' asked Penelope. 'I want to play some Mozart.'

'What's Mozart?' asked Ellie May.

'Classical music,' said Penelope. 'It helps stimulate the brain waves. Makes you feel alive, Clive!'

'Mozart's lovely,' said Fleur.

'Who's Clive?' asked Ellie May.

'Right, your towel's heating up,' said Jeffrey. 'Now, Ellie May, what was it that you wanted to talk about? It's not the puppy thing again, is it?'

'No,' said Ellie May. 'It's –'

'Sorry, where did you say the stereo was?' asked Penelope.

'We don't have one,' said Jeffrey. 'But we don't

need a stereo, actually, because . . . because . . .'

'Because?' prompted Penelope.

'Because . . . we make our own music!' cried Jeffrey, waving his arms like the conductor of an invisible orchestra. 'Don't we, Ellie May? *La la la la la*! Sing with me! *La la la la tra la*!'

'Jeffrey,' said Ellie May, 'I really, really need to talk to you about something. In private. It's properly important.'

'Of course,' said Jeffrey. 'Come on, let's –'

Beeeeep! Beeeeep! Beeeeep! Beeeeep!

Everyone clapped their hands over their ears.

'WHAT'S THAT?' shouted Penelope.

'I THINK IT'S THE SMOKE ALARM,' roared Jeffrey.

'I KNOW IT'S THE SMOKE ALARM. I MEAN, WHAT'S MAKING IT GO OFF?' screamed Penelope.

'I DON'T KNOW. HANG ON, YES I DO,' shouted Jeffrey, flapping at the smoke alarm. 'IT'S ELLIE MAY'S TOWEL. IT'S ON FIRE. AAAAAAARGH, GET SOME WATER, QUICK!'

'WHY IS MY TOWEL ON FIRE?' yelled Ellie May.

'I PUT IT IN THE OVEN,' shouted Jeffrey. 'TO MAKE IT HOT. OH, DEAR!'

'HOLD ON,' screeched Penelope. 'THERE WE GO! I'VE PUT IT OUT NOW. SORRY, JEFFREY. I HAD TO USE YOUR ENERGY DRINK.'

'NO, I'M SORRY!' coughed Jeffrey. 'SORRY, EVERYONE! SORRY! SORRY!'

'I think I'm going to go for a little walk,' said Ellie May.

Ellie May drifted sadly across the film set, like a raft drifting across a melancholy sea full of gloomy fish. There was the cameraman, buffing the lens of his camera. There was the sound man, having a listen to something through his headphones. There was the stuntman, driving a monster truck, backwards.

As she gazed at the exquisite scene around her, Ellie May's heart grew as heavy as something a bit heavier than a normal heart – maybe a tub of body lotion, or a baked potato. She loved her set. She loved the big lights and the bustle and excitement of a new film. She loved the smell of paint and the hush when she stepped out in front of the camera. But not today. Today the lights were too bright and the paint was too smelly and Ellie May didn't want anyone to look at her at all.

Ellie May found the trailer she'd been searching for and pattered up the steps, past a sign that read:

PLEASE PLEASE
LEAVE ME ALONE

'Hello,' she called. 'It's Ellie May here. Can I come in?'

'Are you here to ask me to write a load of

extra lines for some stranger you met at the bus stop?' asked the writer.

'No,' said Ellie May. 'I don't catch buses. I'm an incredibly famous film star.'

'Of course you are,' said the writer. 'Silly of me.'

'So I can come in, then?' asked Ellie May.

The writer groaned. 'All right,' he said.

Ellie May slipped inside and shut the door. The writer had changed. Last time she'd seen him, his eyes had been glinty and keen. Now they were weary and dull. His hair was rumpled, his shirt was crumpled, and he smelled of bad temper and coffee.

'You look like you need some fudge cake,' said Ellie May.

'What I need,' said the writer, 'is an idea for my next film.'

'Aren't you writing *Ugly Duckling*?' enquired Ellie May.

'I've pretty much finished working on *Ugly Duckling*,' said the writer. 'Or, at least, I thought I had, until *someone* came in here asking for extra lines to be put in.'

'Me! That was me!' peeped Ellie May.

'Now I'm writing a new script,' said the writer. 'And for that I need total peace and quiet.'

99

'I see,' said Ellie May.

'To be left completely alone,' said the writer.

'Of course,' said Ellie May.

'With absolutely no disturbances,' said the writer. He hunched down low over his computer.

'So, I've got a bit of a problem,' said Ellie May. 'Well, a lot of a problem, really.'

'Really,' said the writer. 'And this has what, exactly, to do with me?'

'You remember that I said I wanted you to put in a part for my lovely new friend Fleur?' asked Ellie May.

'Vividly,' said the writer.

'Well,' said Ellie May, 'she's still my friend and she's still lovely. But the problem is, now she's here, I sort of wish she wasn't.'

'Of course, why not?' said the writer. 'I stay up half the night writing a scene for this girl and now you want to send her home again. What a waste of my time.'

'It's worse than that,' said Ellie May. 'I just made her look bad in front of everyone. I didn't quite mean to, but I couldn't seem to stop myself.'

The writer sighed, a big, scrumply sigh, like a piece of paper being crunched up into a ball. 'Shouldn't you be telling your chaperone this?'

he asked. 'That thin chap with the bow tie?'

'He's, um, busy,' said Ellie May. 'Everyone is busy. Except you.'

'I'm busy! I'm writing!' said the writer.

'What should I do?' asked Ellie May. 'You look wise. Well, you look wrinkly and tired and that's sort of the same as wise, isn't it? In fact you probably have special ancient wisdom that no one else knows about. So, tell me, what should I do?'

'Dunno,' said the writer.

'Oh,' said Ellie May.

'Now,' said the writer, 'if you could please just let me get on with my script . . .'

'Ah, hang on,' said Ellie May. 'You *do* know what I ought to do. You just want me to realise it for myself, don't you? Oooh! You're even wiser than I thought!'

'Uh, yes. That was the plan,' said the writer.

'Hmm. So what is the valuable lesson?' pondered Ellie May. 'Do I . . . go to the director and tell her that I can't share the spotlight with other people after all, and ask for Fleur to be taken off the film? Yes! No. No, that doesn't sound quite right. In that case, I just have to be the person Jeffrey wants me to be. A nice, normal person. Mmm,' said Ellie May. 'That's much better. And once I'm nice

I won't mind sharing my scene with Fleur! Is that what you meant?'

'Yeah, that kind of thing,' said the writer. 'Does this mean that I can get on with my script?'

'Of course,' said Ellie May. 'Now, since you've helped me so much, maybe you'd like me to help you? I've got lots of ideas for films.'

'Please, just go awa–' began the writer. Then he stopped. 'Actually, you know what? Tell me.'

'Really?' chirped Ellie May.

'Yes, really,' said the writer. 'I wouldn't ask if I wasn't desperate. But it seems that I am.'

'Right, here we go,' said Ellie May. 'How's

this? It would be a film all about a girl who is a pirate. She sails her ship out to a hidden cove and digs up a mysterious old casket. And inside, instead of treasure, there's a fairy. And the

fairy says she can have one wish, and so the pirate girl wishes to turn into a princess. And then her wish is granted! She becomes a beautiful princess. And then this prince turns up and they get married and everyone lives happily ever after. There we go. You can use that!'

'I don't think so,' said the writer.

'OK, I've got another one. This one's about science!' cried Ellie May. 'So there's this girl and she's a scientist. The cleverest scientist in the world. And she does this dangerous experiment to turn cake into gold. Only, the experiment goes wrong and instead of making gold, she makes a fairy.

And the fairy is a wishing fairy and she says, "What wish would you like?" and the scientist says, "Can I be a princess?" and the fairy says, "Yes you can," and the scientist turns into a beautiful princess. And then a handsome prince comes along and the prince and princess get married and everyone lives happily ever after.'

'Please stop,' said the writer.

'One more, one more,' said Ellie May. 'This one's totally different. It's about this girl who lives in the countryside. Then her family moves to New York and she's so lonely. She misses her best friend, and the girls at her new school are massively into fashion and won't talk to her. So she saves up to buy one really amazing outfit to wear so the other girls will like her, even though she knows deep down that she should be buying her best friend a birthday present.'

The writer was leaning forwards. 'Go on . . .' he said. 'There might just be something in this.'

'So,' said Ellie May, 'she saves and saves and then the big day comes. She's in her bedroom about to go out and she opens her purse one more time to check she's got enough money. And inside her purse . . . there's a tiny little fairy who can give wishes! So the girl wishes to get turned into a princess and she does. And then she marries a prince and everyone lives happily ever after.'

'Aaaaaaaaargh!' said the writer.

Chapter Five

Ellie May Should Look Pretty

The make-up artist leaned in with her brush, and Ellie May smiled. Today, everything looked better. The pots of eyeshadow twinkled. The wigs curled sweetly on their mannequins and even the cans of hairspray seemed to shine with hope.

Yesterday she had been jealous and selfish

and horrible, but today was another day. A fresh dawn full of bright new beginnings. Well, it was quite grey outside, and the trailer smelled a bit of feet. But still. Today, Ellie May was a Nice Person.

She waved and grinned as Fleur's reflection appeared in the mirror behind her.

'Morning, Fleur!' beamed the make-up artist. 'I'm just going to get Ellie May over with, and then I'll start on you. It's such a treat to get to make up a real-life model! What mascara are you wearing?'

'I'm not wearing any mascara,' said Fleur. 'This is just what my eyelashes look like.'

'But they're so outrageously long!' said the make-up artist, leaning over to peer at Fleur's face, and elbowing Ellie May in the eye.

'Yay!' said Fleur.

Ellie May was very glad that today she was being Nice. If Nasty Ellie May from yesterday had been here, she would have been feeling very, very cross.

'Right,' said the make-up artist. 'That's your face done, Ellie May. Lean back and I'll sort out your hair.'

'I look all shiny and blotchy,' said Ellie May. 'And you've put a spot on my chin.'

'I know I have,' said the make-up artist. 'Stop trying to rub it off.'

'But – yuck! What are you sticking on my head?' cried Ellie May.

'It's grease, for your roots,' said the make-up artist. 'Sit STILL.'

'But I should look pretty!' grumbled Ellie May. 'And you're making me look awful.'

'You're not supposed to look pretty,' said the make-up artist. 'You're starring in a film called *Ugly Duckling*. What did you expect?'

'But you'll make me look nice when I become the swan girl at the end, won't you?' asked Ellie

May anxiously. 'When I go to sleep and make a wish and turn beautiful?' She gazed into the mirror, imagining her glossy hair, her gorgeous make-up, how she'd open her eyes and smile into the camera.

'It's the whole reason I said that I'd be in this film. You won't make my roots greasy for that?'

'What? Sorry, Ellie May, I wasn't listening,' said the make-up artist. 'Anyway, you're done. Now, off you trot. I want to get going on Fleur. Fleur? Come here, you sweet little thing!'

'I think I'll wait outside,' said Ellie May.

Ellie May was scuffing her feet against the camera track as Fleur came bouncing down the steps.

'Ready!' called Fleur. 'Sorry that took so long.

We started talking about face masks and forgot what time it was.'

'Mmm,' said Nice Ellie May.

'We're actually shooting today, aren't we?' giggled Fleur. 'This is it! I'm so excited!'

'Uh,' grunted Nice Ellie May.

'Hi, Ellie May,' called the cameraman, who was polishing the lens of his camera. 'And hello, Fleur! Great to see you again.'

'Hi, Fleur!' called the sound man, who was polishing the handle of his microphone.

'Morning, Fleur!' called the stuntman, who was polishing the belly of a poisonous spider.

'Can I have your autograph?'

Nice Ellie May didn't mind that no one said "great to see you again" to her. Nice Ellie May didn't mind that the stuntman wanted Fleur's autograph. Nice Ellie May nodded and smiled.

'Morning, everyone!' called Fleur. 'You're making that growly noise again, Ellie May. Is your throat OK? Maybe you should have one of these?' The two girls stopped next to a large freezer. 'Yum,' said Fleur. 'Ice creams. I suppose they're for my scene.'

'*Our* scene,' said Ellie May.

'I love ice cream,' said Fleur. 'I don't have it

normally because Penelope says it's bad for my skin.'

Then, Ellie May had an idea.

A tempting idea. A delicious idea. An idea that sang to her like a forbidden, singing fudge cake.

But she wouldn't listen. Not this time.

'Mmmmmm,' said Fleur. 'Ice cream. Maybe I'll ask Penelope if I can have some tonight? I wouldn't get spots from one ice cream, would I?'

Ellie May opened her mouth to be Nice. Only, instead, somehow, she said, 'You should have one now. While Penelope's not here.'

'Oooh,' said Fleur. 'That would be a bit naughty. I might get told off.'

'But there are lots and lots and lots in here,' said Ellie May. 'No one will miss one little ice-cream cone. And I won't let you get into trouble.'

'Well, if you think it's all right . . .' said Fleur doubtfully.

'*I'm* going to,' said Ellie May, reaching into the freezer. 'Oh, look, I've picked up a whole load of them! You should have two, since you like them so much.'

'Thank you,' said Fleur. 'And I get to eat one later on, don't I? It says so in the script. I wonder why they've got so many? Maybe it's to give everyone else one when we've finished.'

'Yes, that'll be it,' said Ellie May.

'Yum!' said Fleur. 'What a lovely day!'

'Yum yum,' said Ellie May. 'Why stop at two ice creams? Have four! There we go, Fleur. Have all the ice cream you can eat! What a lovely day.'

'Hello, girls,' said the director. 'Ready to shoot your scene? I hope you like ice cream, Fleur. You're going to be eating lots of it.'

'I love ice cream,' said Fleur.

'So,' said the director. 'Ellie May, you're buying your ice cream. Fleur, ready to grab it off her? Great. Places, please.'

'More ice cream!' cried Fleur. 'Yay!'

'OK, so, off we go,' said the director. '*Ugly Ducking*, scene five, take one. Action!'

Ellie May leaned up to the ice-cream van window. 'Mint choc chip, please,' she said.

Fleur stalked across the set and snatched the cone away.

'But that's mine!' stuttered Ellie May.

'Oh, dear, did I push in front of you?' jeered Fleur. She took a big bite of the ice cream. 'You're so plain and boring that I didn't even notice you were here!'

'And cut!' called the director. 'Great. A fantastic performance once again, Fleur. Ellie May, you were fine, but a little more focus, please? Right, let's reset for the wide shot.'

Fleur tugged at Ellie May's arm. 'Aren't we finished?' she asked.

'No, we might have to do it maybe a couple

more times,' said Ellie May.

'It's just, I'm feeling a bit weird,' said Fleur. 'Maybe it's all the ice cream. I didn't know we'd have to do it more than once.'

'Oh, look,' said Ellie May. 'You've got some ice cream on your face.'

'Here?' Fleur rubbed her cheek. 'Has it gone?'

'No, it's sort of up by your eye,' said Ellie May. 'There you go. That's got it.'

'Right,' said the director. '*Ugly Duckling*, take – hold on, Fleur, your make-up's all smudged. Can someone come and fix it please?'

The make-up artist ran over to dab at Fleur's

eye, while Ellie May shook herself. What was she doing? This wasn't how today was supposed to go.

'There we are, poppet,' said the make-up artist, giving Fleur's arm a squeeze. 'All better. You're doing ever so well, you really are.'

'My turn,' said Ellie May, lifting her chin for a brush or two of powder, but the make-up artist swept past her and was gone.

'Ready to go again, girls?' called the director.

'I think so,' said Fleur. She leaned in to Ellie May. 'I'm not enjoying this as much as I thought I would,' she whispered.

'Well, acting isn't for everyone,' said Ellie May.

'Oh,' she added lightly, 'maybe, try not to blink so much. The very best actors never blink at all.'

'No blinking. OK,' said Fleur.

'And we're going for the wide,' said the director. '*Ugly Duckling*, scene five, take two. Action!'

Ellie May leaned up to the ice-cream van window. 'Mint choc chip, please,' she said.

Fleur stalked across the set, her eyes staring hard, and snatched the cone away.

'But that's mine!' stuttered Ellie May.

'Oh, dear, did I push in front of you?' jeered Fleur, her eyes almost popping out of her head. She took a big bite of the ice cream. 'You're so plain and boring that I

didn't even notice you were here!'

'Um, OK, I'm not sure what you were doing with your eyes there, Fleur, but never mind,' said the director. 'Let's do that one more time, shall we, and then we'll set up for the aerial shot.'

'I don't seem to be doing as well as I was before,' said Fleur. 'You will keep helping me, won't you, Ellie May?'

'Of course!' said Ellie May. 'I've got lots more useful advice. Lots and lots and lots. Don't worry, Fleur. You just listen to me and things will start getting better very soon.'

But . . .

'What are you looking up there for, Fleur?' said the director. 'Take nine!'

and

'Don't change the lines, Fleur. Take fourteen!'

and

'No, we're not doing this scene standing on one leg, Fleur. Take twenty!'

and

'Remember, Fleur, you really want to eat Ellie May's ice cream. You don't look like you're enjoying it any more.'

'Urg,' said Fleur.

'Right, in for the close-up,' said the director.

'*Ugly Duckling*, scene five, take twenty-one. And – action!'

Ellie May leaned up to the ice-cream van window.
'*Mint choc chip, please,*' *she said.*

Fleur lurched across the set and took the cone away.

'*But that's mine!*' *stuttered Ellie May.*

'*Oh, dear, did I push in front of you?*' *gulped Fleur. She took a teeny tiny little bite of the ice cream.*

'And cut,' said the director. 'Fleur. Is something wrong?'

'I think I'm going to be sick,' said Fleur. She put her pretty hand over her pretty mouth, made a not-very-pretty noise and scampered off in the direction of the toilets.

'Poor Fleur,' said Ellie May. 'How unprofessional.'

'Oh, dear,' sighed the director. 'Can someone go and check she's OK?' The stuntman untangled himself from the lion he was taming and rushed off after her.

'Right,' said the director, 'I suppose we might as well make a start on your scene, then, Ellie May.'

'OK!' beamed Ellie May.

'Yes, but don't look too cheerful about it,' said the director. 'This is supposed to be a sad moment.'

'Of course,' said Ellie May, tilting her face up for the make-up artist to apply a little blusher to her cheeks. 'And look! My skin is really glowing.'

'Is it?' asked the make-up artist.

'Yes,' said Ellie May. 'I think you'll find it is. And I'd like you to know that my eyelashes are totally natural.'

'No one's saying they're not,' said the

make-up artist.

Ellie May walked to the middle of the set and stood right in front of the camera. 'Now,' she said, 'how would you like me to do this scene? Because I'm extremely talented and experienced and I can play it any way you want.'

'Just the way you normally do it will be fine, thanks,' said the director. 'Ah, you're back, Fleur. What a relief! We were all a bit worried about you, you poor mite. Have you got everything you need? Sit down at the side there with a glass of water while we get Ellie May's scene out of the way, then we'll come back to you.'

'There's a funny noise coming over the microphones,' said the sound man. 'It's almost like someone's growling.'

'Ellie May!' called Fleur. 'You *are* allowed to blink when you're acting. Even the best actors blink sometimes. Cassie Craven blinks all the time! The stuntman just told me and I thought you'd want to know.'

Ellie May knew she shouldn't reply. She knew she should shut her mouth tight and get on with her scene. But she just couldn't. Something was burning deep inside her where all the good parts were supposed to be. Something hot and sharp and mean.

Ellie May turned slowly to Fleur, and said, 'I know.'

'You know?' repeated Fleur.

'Yes,' said Ellie May. 'It's very kind of you to try to help me, but I really don't need any advice from you. I think we have to remember which one of us is only a model and which one is an incredibly famous film star.'

For a moment, Fleur was silent. Then, she said, 'I don't understand. If you knew that it was OK to blink, then why did you tell me that I shouldn't?'

The film set had never been so quiet. Not when the sound man had shouted, 'Quiet!' Not when the director had lost her voice. Not when they'd been filming *Silent Night: A Life in Mime,* in the scene that was set in a library.

Fleur frowned. 'It doesn't make sense,' she muttered. 'It must have been a mistake. Mustn't it? Only . . . even if it was, why did you let me eat all that ice cream? You knew that we'd have to do the scene lots of times but you didn't tell me.' Fleur shook her head. 'Did you . . . did you *want* me to be sick?'

Ellie May dropped her head, her cheeks growing hotter by the second.

'And . . .' Fleur gasped, 'oh, Ellie May, you

made me smudge my make-up and you told me to stare at the wrong spot and it was you who changed my lines and . . .' Fleur's eyes were gleaming with tears, 'and you had me trying not to blink and standing on one leg . . . *and* you gave me hiccups!'

Ellie May gazed down at the ground.

'You wanted me to look bad, didn't you?' whispered Fleur. 'But why? Why would you get me to be in your film and then make me mess it all up?'

Ellie May shifted from foot to foot as Fleur stared. The director stared. The sound man stared.

The cameraman stared. The stuntman stared, and the lion he was taming stared, too, even though it didn't know why it was staring, because it was a lion.

'I didn't ask to be in *Ugly Duckling*,' said Fleur. 'You asked me! And now you're being horrible. Did I do something to upset you? If I did, I didn't mean to. I thought . . . I thought we were friends.'

Ellie May opened her mouth but no answer came out. Instead, she burst into tears.

The director got to her feet. 'Right, that's it.'

Ellie May cried harder.

'This morning has been a total disaster,' said

the director. 'I just can't have this kind of behaviour. In case you hadn't noticed, we're here to make a film.'

Ellie May could only sob.

'This isn't a game, it isn't a playground, we are working,' said the director. 'We do not have time for this.'

'I know!' howled Ellie May.

'Good,' said the director.

'It won't happen again,' choked Ellie May.

'No, it won't,' said the director. 'I won't have these hysterics on my set. I've made my decision.'

'Please . . .' whispered Ellie May.

139

'I'm sorry,' said the director.

'But . . .' pleaded Ellie May.

'No buts,' said the director. 'Fleur, you're fired.'

'Wha–' began Ellie May.

'So dry your eyes, Ellie May!' exclaimed the director. 'We need to keep our little superstar nice and cheerful.'

'But I thought you would fire *me*,' cried Ellie May.

'Fire you? I'd have to be mad!' said the director. 'You're the whole reason people will be coming to see this film! So, no more tantrums. From now on it's going to be all about you.

Someone get a chaperone and have Fleur escorted back to her trailer, please? And make-up, could you sort out Ellie May's face? No no, don't worry, we can lose that scene easily enough. I'll get the writer to have another look at the script tonight. Come on, Ellie May, enough of all this crying. The show must go on!'

But Ellie May couldn't stop. She wept and wept, as her new friend was gently, gently led away.

Chapter Six

Ellie May is Not Finished Yet

The lake was very peaceful. Sunshine glimmered peacefully upon the water. Dragonflies danced peacefully in the sky. Fifty-six people peacefully set up four lorries' worth of equipment. A generator peacefully clunked and helicopters hovered peacefully overhead.

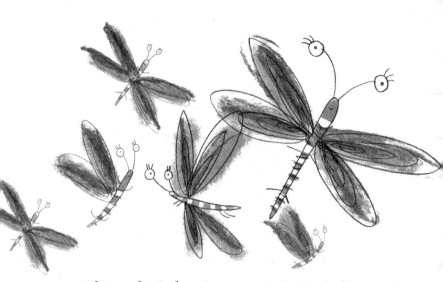

'Ah,' sighed the director. 'I do love filming on location. There's really nothing like it!'

'I agree,' said the sound man, setting up his microphone.

'Me too,' said the cameraman, adjusting his camera.

'Eeeeaaaaargh!' said the stuntman, who was being run over by a speedboat.

☆ 143 ☆

'How long until we start?' asked Ellie May.

'Another few minutes, I think,' said the director. 'Why don't you talk to the crew while we finish setting up the lights?'

Ellie May turned hopefully to the film crew.

'I'm busy, actually,' said the sound man.

'Me too,' said the cameraman.

'Oh,' said Ellie May. She smiled at the stuntman. 'Maybe you could show me how to swallow swords again? That's always fun.'

'I'm busy too,' said the stuntman. 'I'm being run over by a speedboat, in case you hadn't noticed.'

144

'Sorry,' said Ellie May softly. 'I thought you'd finished.'

'Hey, Ellie May!' called Jeffrey, who was stretched out on a picnic rug. 'Come and sit with me! I'm reading this book on hypnotism that Penelope lent me. It's all about how to become the very best person you can be.' He turned slowly from page to page. 'You just relax and let your whole body grow heavy, from your feet, up through your knees . . . to your chest . . . letting all the tension drain away . . . just drain away . . . until your eyes close . . . and then . . . you . . . go . . . to . . . sleeeep . . .'

'Maybe in a bit,' said Ellie May. She gazed out across the shimmering water.

'Yes!' called the director. 'That's exactly the look we want for this scene, Ellie May. Solitary and sad. Like you're completely alone in the world and no one cares about you at all. Perfect!'

Ellie May tossed her hair. She was sick of being solitary. She was sick of being sad. And she was especially sick of no one caring about her at all.

'All right,' she said. 'What is it?'

'What's what?' asked the cameraman.

'You're all ignoring me,' asked Ellie May. 'You've been doing it for days and days and days and I think it's really horrible of you.'

'Well, you were horrible to Fleur,' said the cameraman.

'But I didn't mean to be,' said Ellie May.

'It didn't look like that from where I was,' said the cameraman. 'And I was watching you very carefully. Through my camera.'

'But if you'd listened . . .' Ellie May began.

'I was listening,' said the sound man. 'I was

listening through my headphones. You were really unpleasant.'

Ellie May gave in. 'I know I was,' she said miserably. 'I can't help it. I tried not to be but I'm just a nasty person. Anyway, there's nothing I can do about it now, is there?'

'You can say you're sorry,' said the sound man.

'Yeah,' said the cameraman.

'Blwblwblwblwa,' said the stuntman, who had just that moment gone underwater.

'Maybe . . .' said Ellie May doubtfully. 'But . . .'

'You *are* sorry, aren't you?' said the cameraman.

'Of course I'm sorry!' cried Ellie May. 'I feel

terrible! Which is why I've been trying to forget all about it.'

'We haven't forgotten,' said the sound man. 'And I don't think that Fleur will have forgotten, either.'

'No . . .' said Ellie May. 'No, I suppose not.'

The generator clunked. The helicopters whirred. The lake just sat there.

'You're right,' sighed Ellie May. 'I should say sorry. I *will* say sorry. I just hope that Fleur will forgive me.'

'OK!' said the cameraman.

'Good girl,' said the sound man. 'It's the

right thing to do.'

'Now, then,' said the director. 'Back to work. So here's our shot: Ellie May, on her own, looking out across the lake. Rats, now the sun's gone in. Can someone put a spotlight on to her face, please? Right, here we go. *Ugly Duckling*, scene eighteen, take one. And – action.'

Ellie May tapped the microphone. 'Is this working?' she asked.

'Try saying something,' said the sound man.

'One two one two Ellie May Ellie May Ellie May,' said Ellie May.

'Yup, you're on,' said the sound man. 'Everything else all right?

'It's great, thank you,' replied Ellie May. She beamed. 'The lighting is perfect. And those flowers are a nice touch. It's a shame they're not real ones, but I'm sure Fleur will understand.'

'And you don't think it's a bit over the top?' asked the director.

'No, I don't. I want to get this apology absolutely right,' said Ellie May. 'It's the very least that she deserves. Now, can the violinists get behind me? Tallest at the back, shortest at the front. Thank you.'

'She's coming! She's coming!' cried the cameraman.

'OK!' cried Ellie May. 'Everyone in their places, please!'

The whole crew had gathered together. The sound man was there, holding his microphone. The cameraman was there, holding his camera. The stuntman was there, holding a burning motorbike.

And, just behind them, there was a car, holding a small, uncertain girl, with eyes the colour of a swimming pool on an uncertain day.

'Hello, everyone,' said Fleur.

'Hello, Fleur!' cried the film crew.

Ellie May paused and cleared her throat. This was it. Any second now and everything would be all right. Fleur would smile and the film crew would clap and that nasty sharp feeling in her chest would turn soft and fluffy and good.

She reached for her friend's hand, and led her through all the people. The violins began to play. Everyone watched and waited.

'I-I just wanted to say,' Ellie May stuttered, 'that I am very sorry.'

'Aw,' said the director. 'That's sweet.'

'I was mean to you, Fleur,' said Ellie May, 'and it was wrong.'

'It's OK,' said Fleur.

'No, it isn't OK,' insisted Ellie May. 'It was my idea for you to come here, and I should have been nice.'

'It's all right, really,' said Fleur.

'It really isn't,' said Ellie May. 'You are so pretty and so good at acting that I got jealous. Which I shouldn't have done, because I'm pretty and good at acting as well. But even though I'm at least as good as you are, I let that jealousy destroy our precious friendship.' She frowned. Even though the words had sounded fine in her head, now she heard them out loud, they didn't seem quite right.

'But you didn't mean to do it,' said Fleur.

'Sometimes,' said Ellie May, deciding to ignore the strange sensation in her stomach and carry on, 'I need to realise that life isn't all about me. It's about other people as well. But it's hard, when you're famous.'

'I understand –' began Fleur.

'I'm not sure you do,' said Ellie May.

'Why not?' asked Fleur.

'No one really understands,' said Ellie May. 'Because no one else is as famous as me.'

156

'I'm a bit famous,' said Fleur. 'So I sort of do.'

'You think you do,' said Ellie May. 'But in the end, you don't.'

'Oh,' said Fleur.

'The thing is, when you're as incredibly famous as I am, you get used to being the centre of attention and it's hard to remember to share,' said Ellie May, turning slowly towards the audience of onlookers. 'I need to learn to fade into the background. I need to learn to put others before myself, however painful, however hard . . .'

'Is this a bit from one of her films?' muttered the sound man.

Ellie May flung her arms into the air.

'I know I'm not perfect,' she cried. 'I'm far

from being perfect. Maybe too far. But –'

'It's OK!' said Fleur.

'Shh, I'm not finished yet,' said Ellie May. 'Where was I? Fade into the background . . . put others before myself . . . Oh, yes. I know I'm not perfect. I'm far from being perfect. Maybe too far. But I hope, if you look into your heart, perhaps, one day, you'll find a way to forgive me.' She twisted round to the violinists. 'Can you please hush down a bit?'

The violins hushed.

'I'm finished now,' said Ellie May. 'Well, Fleur?'

'I already told you, it's all right,' said Fleur.

'Ah,' said Ellie May.

'Yes,' said Fleur.

'Good,' said Ellie May.

'So . . . I suppose . . . I'll go, then,' said Fleur.

'Bye bye, Fleur,' said Ellie May.

The crowd parted around Fleur as she made her way back to the car. The door slammed with a hollow thump. The engine started with a hollow roar. And then the car drove away with Fleur inside, which was only possible because it was hollow.

Ellie May turned back to the film crew. 'Hooray,' she said. 'All better now. So, shall we get on with shooting the next scene?'

The sound man slowly lowered his

microphone. 'No,' he said. 'I don't think we shall.'

The cameraman put down his camera.

'But I said I was sorry,' moaned Ellie May. 'So what's the problem?'

'That was a terrible apology,' said the cameraman. 'Probably the worst apology I've ever seen.'

'It was the worst apology I've ever heard,' agreed the sound man. 'It wasn't about Fleur's feelings. It was all about you.'

'But it *is* all about me,' said Ellie May. 'I was the one who was nasty, after all.'

'And where was the part where you asked Fleur to come back to *Ugly Duckling*?' asked the sound man. 'What happened to that?'

'That's not fair!' protested Ellie May. 'You never told me I had to ask Fleur back to the film! I was listening very carefully because it was important and you really never said that. You just said I should say sorry and I did. So stop being mean! I've done what you wanted. You should be nice to me!'

'Why should we?' said the stuntman. 'We don't think you deserve it.'

'It doesn't matter what you think!' cried Ellie May wildly, 'because I'm the star of this film! Not Fleur and not you. Me!'

'It's like that, is it?' said the stuntman. 'Well, fine.' He threw the burning motorbike to the ground. 'I quit.'

The cameraman switched off his camera. 'Me too,' he said.

'Me three,' said the sound man. 'I don't want to make a film with you any more, Ellie May.'

'But . . .' said Ellie May. 'But . . .'

The director shut her eyes. 'That's it then,' she said. '*Ugly Duckling* is over.'

Chapter Seven

Ellie May Does Not Want a Healing Crystal

Darkness was falling. It fell upon the abandoned cameras. It fell upon the empty film set. It fell upon the backdrop, which swung in the wind, like the sail of a boat. Not a jolly, cheerful boat, but a sad, empty boat, sailing away on an ocean of tears with a cargo of despair.

Ellie May tried sitting in the chair that said DIRECTOR on the back. Then she went and picked up a camera. Ellie May had always wanted to know what it was like to look through a film camera. She peered in. All she could see were great expanses of space where people should have been, but weren't.

Ellie May rested the camera back down on the ground. She stepped over the sound man's microphone and across to the painted door of the sweet shop, and let her fingers trail across the handle. And perhaps it was the emptiness and silence, or maybe it was the chill of the night air, but Ellie May began to shiver.

There was a light on back in her trailer. Jeffrey would be there. Kind, gentle Jeffrey, ready to take her home. Ellie May hesitated and then turned away.

One other light was on. A light in a trailer with a sign on the door that read:

DON'T EVEN THINK ABOUT COMING IN UNLESS YOU WANT ME TO SHOUT AT YOU!

She knocked with a trembling fist.

'Go away!' called the writer.

'You don't mean me, though,' said Ellie May, sliding inside.

'I really do,' said the writer.

'That joke is getting a bit old now,' said Ellie May. 'You should probably think of a better one.'

The writer turned around in his chair. He looked worse than ever. His hair was lank, his skin was grey and his chin had started to grow a beard but then given up halfway through.

'Help me?' said Ellie May. 'I'm a bit desperate, actually. You will help me, won't you?'

'Er –' began the writer.

'Phew,' said Ellie May, settling down on the sofa. 'Right, first things first. I'm feeling a bit shaky, so could you please make me a cup of tea?'

By the time Ellie May returned to her own trailer, the darkness was so velvety black that she couldn't even see her hands in front of her face. Although that could have been because she was wearing black velvet gloves.

'There you are!' cried Jeffrey. 'I was worried.

Come on, everything's all packed up. We can go home.'

'What's that smell?' sniffed Ellie May.

'I've been burning some of Penelope's essential oils,' said Jeffrey. 'This is a mixture of jasmine and ylang-ylang.'

'Ywhat-ywhat?' asked Ellie May.

'Ylang-ylang,' said Jeffrey. 'It's to make you feel calm and happy. Do you feel calm and happy, Ellie May?'

Ellie May considered for a moment. 'No,' she said. 'Which is weird, because I've got some good news.'

170

'Really?' asked Jeffrey. 'That's fantastic! What is it?'

'The writer just told me about this film by a friend of his. It's called *Horsing Around* and it's all about horses and shooting starts next week but their lead actress has broken her leg. She fell off a horse. Anyway, he reckons I can be in that instead, if I want. So, you see, it doesn't matter about *Ugly Duckling*. It doesn't matter at all.'

Ellie May looked at Jeffrey.

Jeffrey looked at Ellie May.

'Great,' said Jeffrey.

'Great,' said Ellie May.

'So . . .' said Jeffrey, 'do you want a healing crystal? You can hang it round your neck.'

'No, thank you,' said Ellie May.

'Some goji berries?' said Jeffrey. 'I have loads.'

Ellie May shook her head.

'How about a sit in a flotation tank?' asked Jeffrey. 'Or you could wear this special bracelet that pushes on pressure points in your wrists, or maybe try some reiki or . . . Ellie May, you're crying.'

'I don't understand,' wept Ellie May. 'I thought I liked it that my films were all about me. And I do. I really like it. So why do I miss everyone?'

'Oh, Ellie May,' murmured Jeffrey.

'I miss them all,' sniffed Ellie May. 'I miss the cameraman and the sound man and the stuntman and the make-up artist . . . and . . . I . . . miss . . . Fleur!'

Jeffrey stroked Ellie May's hair until her sobs began to slow.

'I don't want to be in *Horsing Around*,' whispered Ellie May. 'I want to be in *Ugly Duckling*. With my friends. Only . . . they're not my friends any more.'

'But they could be,' said Jeffrey, wiping her face with his spotted handkerchief, 'if you told them what you just told me.'

'Really?' murmured Ellie May. 'Do you really really think so?'

'I know so,' said Jeffrey, holding out the handkerchief. 'Now, blow.'

'Then in that case,' snuffled Ellie May, 'I have to go and see the director. Will you come with me?'

'Of course I will,' said Jeffrey. 'Do you want to listen to a bit of opera before you go? To put you in the right mood?'

'To be honest,' said Ellie May, 'it puts me in the right mood just being with you. This is much better than going to see the writer.'

'Does the writer offer you a mud wrap with

real mud in it?' asked Jeffrey.

'No,' said Ellie May.

'And would you like a mud wrap?' asked Jeffrey. 'Or an energy drink?'

'I don't think I want a mud wrap,' said Ellie May. 'And I definitely don't want an energy drink. But thank you anyway.'

'Then what would you like?' said Jeffrey. 'What would you like most of all?'

'A puppy?' asked Ellie May hopefully.

'Other than a puppy,' said Jeffrey.

'I think,' said Ellie May, 'that I like it most when we just sit and talk. Like this.'

Jeffrey sighed a long sigh. It was a sigh full of hot towels and goji berries and Mozart and wheatgrass. 'Of course you do,' he said. 'Of course you do. Now, wash your face and then we'll go and find the director.'

Ellie May lifted her head from her chaperone's tweedy jacket. 'Oh, Jeffrey,' she said, 'I wish I'd come to you sooner. The writer was nice, but he's not you. In fact, and you must promise me that you won't tell anyone, but sometimes I find him a little bit irritating.'

'Knock knock!' said Ellie May.

'No,' said the writer.

'You're supposed to say, "Who's there?"' said Ellie May.

'*No*,' said the writer.

'It's, "Who's . . ." oh, never mind, we're coming in!' called Ellie May.

She stepped into the writer's trailer, past a sign that read:

WHAT IS tHE POINT OF
THIS SIGN? NO ONE WILL
BotHER TO READ IT
La La LA LA
BottOMS

The writer looked dreadful. In fact, he looked worse than dreadful. He looked . . .

'What's a word that means "worse than dreadful"?' wondered Ellie May.

'Don't ask me,' said the writer. 'I don't know. I'm a terrible writer.'

'How's your new script going?' asked Jeffrey. 'Did you come up with an idea, in the end? Ellie May said you were having trouble.'

The writer put his head in his hands.

'Hello?' said a voice from the doorway.

'Who is it now?' howled the writer.

'The director,' said the director. 'What's the occasion, Ellie May? Why aren't you on your way home?'

'Thanks for coming,' said Ellie May. 'I invited you all here because I need you to help me.'

'What do you mean, "Thanks for coming"? This is *my* trailer,' said the writer.

'Cup of tea, anyone?' asked Jeffrey. 'And maybe a bit of cake? Gosh, it's a bit of a mess in here! Now, where are the plates . . .?'

'It's about *Ugly Duckling*,' said Ellie May.

'*Ugly Duckling* is finished,' said the director.

'Yes, well, no, actually,' said Ellie May. She glanced over to Jeffrey, who gave her an encouraging smile. 'I've decided . . . I think . . .'

Ellie May scrunched her eyes shut and talked very fast before the words could get stuck.

'I was wondering whether we could put Fleur's ice-cream scene back in? I want to show everyone I'm truly sorry for what I did. So I thought we could do it again. And I'll be nice this time. I promise.'

There.

She'd said it.

Ellie May opened her eyes and waited.

'Oh, Ellie May,' said the director, 'it's far too late for that now.'

'Wh-what do you mean?' stuttered Ellie May.

'We've lost so much time already. Even if we could get the crew back, the one thing we definitely can't do is reshoot a scene we've already cut out. I wish I didn't have to say this but I'm afraid that *Ugly Duckling* really is over.'

'But –' began Ellie May desperately. 'I have to

make it up to her . . . I need them to know . . . please? Please!'

'I'm so sorry,' said the director, and she looked it. Even the writer seemed sad. Not in his normal, writery way, but a new kind of sadness, as though he cared for Ellie May and was upset that she was so unhappy. But Ellie May could have been wrong about that.

Jeffrey took her by the shoulders and guided her to one side.

'It's all right,' he said. 'You did the right thing just now, and it wasn't your fault that it was too late. We'll get going on that horse film next week, and

183

there'll be a new crew and new actors and you'll be nice to them this time. Lesson learned and a clean slate and all that. Smile, Ellie May! It's going to be OK. We'll turn this into something good. You'll see.'

'Turn . . .' said Ellie May slowly. 'Turn . . . into something . . . good . . .'

She remembered Fleur.

Fleur, who was the same height as Ellie May, and had the same colour hair. Fleur, who was just like Ellie May, only prettier. Fleur, the girl everyone loved. Fleur, who was good.

And suddenly Ellie May knew what she should do. What she ought to do. What she *had* to do, if only she could bear it.

'Let's go home then,' said Jeffrey, 'and put all this behind us. Come on, Ellie May. There's nothing more we can do here.'

Ellie May hesitated, just for a moment. Then she lifted her chin.

'Actually,' she said, 'there is one more thing we

can do. Pass me some fudge cake, please, Jeffrey? Now listen, everyone, because I've just had an amazingly amazing idea . . .'

Chapter Eight

Ellie May is Incredibly Famous. And Nice

Ellie May lay curled in bed beneath her window. The moonlight shone upon her greasy hair and spotty chin as her lips moved.

'I wish . . .' murmured the sleeping girl. 'I wish . . . I could be beautiful.'

And then something strange began to happen. Perhaps the stars had heard her pleas. Perhaps wishes really do come true. Or perhaps it was the magic of cinema, and computers, but as the silvery beams bathed the girl's face, she began to transform. Slowly . . . slowly . . . the spot on her chin vanished. Her murmuring lips turned rosy pink. Her nose shrank and her neck lengthened and her greasy hair grew rich and lustrous.

As the sun's first rays kissed her cheeks, the girl opened her eyes and they were the blue of a swimming pool on the very first day of summer.

She touched her face, then, throwing off the bed sheets, she ran to the mirror.

'But . . . I'm not an ugly duckling any more!' whispered Fleur. 'I'm beautiful!'

The bedroom door swung open and suddenly the room was crowded with little girls who all happened to be passing for some reason.

'Hooray!' cried the little girls, rushing up to give her a cuddle. 'Now you're beautiful, we all like you and we want to be your friends!'

'I'm really not sure about the moral message of this film,' muttered Jeffrey.

'So, what do you think?' asked Ellie May anxiously, as the credits began to roll. 'Did you like it? How was I?'

'You were great!' said Jeffrey. 'Really fantastic.'

'I thought so,' said Ellie May. She smiled a satisfied smile. 'It's nice to sit in the cinema and watch it properly. With popcorn. And fudge cake. You'd think I would get bored of seeing me up there –'

'I wouldn't, actually,' said Jeffrey.

'– but in fact,' said Ellie May, 'I never, ever do.'

'Well, we're all incredibly happy,' said the director. 'And that transformation scene, oh, Ellie May, you made absolutely the right decision.'

'I know,' said Ellie May.

'Yay!' said Fleur.

The lights came up, and Ellie May could see the whole film crew. The cameraman was smiling. The sound man was smiling. And the stuntman, who was dangling from the ceiling, put out his arm and gave her a big thumbs up.

'Well done, Fleur,' said Ellie May. 'You were properly brilliant.'

'Really?' asked Fleur.

'Truly,' said Ellie May. 'I'm so glad you're in *Ugly Duckling* with me. What? Why are you looking at me like that? Have I got cake on my face?'

191

'No. Well, a bit. But . . . just . . . I thought that maybe you were asking me to be the swan girl because you had to, to save the film,' said Fleur. 'I didn't think you *wanted* me to be in it.'

'I did! I do!' cried

Ellie May. 'I was trying to save

the film, of course. But I've loved having you in

it with me.'

Fleur blushed. 'You're a really nice person,' she said.

'That's just normal old me,' said Ellie May, picking up her sunglasses and her bag and her hat and her back-up hat.

'I don't think you're normal,' said Fleur.

Ellie May's grin faded a little. 'What do you mean?' she asked.

'I think you're completely wonderful,' said Fleur. 'I've always wanted to be in a film, and now I am. My dream came true, and it was thanks to you, Ellie May.'

Jeffrey slipped from his seat and walked towards the cinema lobby. There might just be time to nip out and pick up the new edition of *Giggle* before Ellie May decided she wanted to go home.

A thin, pointy woman rushed by. And stopped.

'J-man,' she said.

'Penelope!' cried Jeffrey. 'How marvellous to see you! You're looking . . .'

Penelope looked rather tired and worried.

'You're looking terrific!' said Jeffrey. 'So, how's it going?'

'Fine,' said Penelope. 'Better than fine, actually. Fleur's been really busy. She's never had so much work before! I think it must have been all the publicity from *Ugly Duckling*. Everyone wants her photo.'

'But that's brilliant!' said Jeffrey.

'Yes,' said Penelope. 'And – newsflash! – we've just started doing pilates. It makes a nice change from yoga and tai chi. Oh, I meant to tell you, I'm having major success with this new energy drink. I put oats in and . . . oh, who am I kidding?'

'Er, I don't know,' said Jeffrey. 'Phil? Clive? Stan?'

'Jeffrey, I'm hopeless at this,' sighed Penelope. 'It was one thing, doing the odd job together here and there, but now we're together day in, day out, something's changed. Fleur's gone right off my granola bars and she never wants to listen to Mozart any more. I've tried art therapy and herbal therapy and fish therapy . . . but none of it has really worked. I'm a terrible chaperone!'

'No!' cried Jeffrey. 'I have to tell you, I've been in awe of you ever since we met. You're terrific! Fish therapy? Yowzers.'

'No, you're terrific!' said Penelope.

'No, you are!' insisted Jeffery.

'No, *you* are,' said Penelope. 'I saw you with Ellie May today. She's happy. She trusts you. That's what

I want for me and Fleur. What's your secret?'

'I don't really have one,' said Jeffrey.

'But what do you do when you're together?' asked Penelope.

'We just . . . we just talk to each other,' said Jeffrey. 'She talks and I listen. Sometimes we swap around for a bit.'

'Talking!' said Penelope. 'Listening! Fab! We can do that! In fact, I found this great interactive game a few days ago where each person says something and then a light goes on and you swap seats and –'

'No,' said Jeffrey. 'Just ordinary talking and

listening. Like we are now.'

'That's really *all*?' said Penelope.

Jeffrey shrugged. 'Yup, that's all.' He gazed at Penelope's dejected face. 'Well,' he said, 'I suppose it's not quite all. There is one thing you can do.'

'I knew it!' exclaimed Penelope. 'There *is* a secret! Tell me, Jeffrey? I won't share it with anyone else, I promise.'

'The secret,' grinned Jeffrey, 'and this is just between you and me, Penelope, but the secret is a really good recipe for fudge cake.'

Ellie May walked with Jeffrey back to the car. 'So,' she began. 'Everyone's saying how good Fleur was.'

'Really?' said Jeffrey carefully. 'And what do you think?'

'I thought she was amazingly amazing,' said Ellie May. 'Definitely as good as I would have been in that part. In fact, maybe she was even better? Hmm. Actually, I'm not sure she was quite *that* amazing. But she was certainly very good. I'm so glad we saw it together and I got to say "well done".'

'I do think that you're being awfully nice

about all this,' said Jeffrey. 'It takes huge strength of character to be the kind of person that you were just now. I've seen how far you've come and I couldn't be more proud of you. You've stopped wanting to be the centre of attention all the time! You're really not jealous of Fleur at all!'

Ellie May's shoes crunched across the gravel of the car park.

'I am,' said Ellie May.

'You are what?' asked Jeffrey.

'Jealous of Fleur,' said Ellie May. 'I was jealous of her when we came into the cinema and I saw her on the posters.'

'Oh,' said Jeffrey.

'And then, when I turned into her at the end, I was so jealous that I thought I might cry,' said Ellie May.

'Ah,' said Jeffrey.

'And when her name came up on the credits next to mine I was so jealous that I thought I might scream!' said Ellie May.

'So . . .'

'All that, just now, it was acting,' explained Ellie May. 'Well, not quite all of it. Because I'm jealous of Fleur and happy for her at the same time. Like how there's fudge and cake in fudge cake at the same time.'

'I see,' said Jeffrey.

'And I've tried ever so hard,' said Ellie May, 'but I don't think I can stop being jealous altogether. Does that mean that I'm not a nice person after all?'

Ellie May's shoes went *crunch crunch crunch*.

'It means that you are an extra-nice person, Ellie May,' said Jeffrey.

'Really?' said Ellie May.

'Absolutely!' said Jeffrey. 'You were feeling jealous and you still managed to do the right thing. That's what being a nice person is all about.'

'Wow!' said Ellie May happily. 'And if I even had you convinced that I didn't mind having Fleur in *Ugly Duckling* with me, then I must be a really brilliant actress, mustn't I? One of the best ones that's ever lived. As well as being incredibly famous. And nice.'

'Er, yes,' said Jeffrey, opening the car door. 'So. Look. I've been thinking. It's a bit impractical, but . . . you can have a puppy if you really, really want one. You've earned it.'

'Seriously?' breathed Ellie May.

'Yes, seriously,' said Jeffrey. 'So long as you promise to feed it –'

'I will!' cried Ellie May.

'And walk it,' said Jeffrey.

'Of course!' shrieked Ellie May.

'And pick up all its poo,' said Jeffrey.

'Um,' said Ellie May. 'I just wonder if, maybe, I'm a bit busy to have a puppy, right now. What with all the acting I'm doing. What a shame. Oh, well.'

Jeffrey smiled. 'So, have you thought about which film you'll do next, then?' he asked. 'I'm sure you can have a part in *Green With Jealousy*, if you want. It's by the writer of *Ugly Duckling* and I know how much he likes you.'

'I'm glad he managed to think of an idea,' said Ellie May. 'What happens in it?'

'It's all about two girls who are friends,' said Jeffrey. 'Then one girl gets jealous of the other one and does horrible things to make her look bad.

But they work it out in the end.'

'But when do the girls go green?' asked Ellie May. 'And why?'

'It's not . . . I don't know . . .' began Jeffrey.

'Then you must have missed something out,' said Ellie May. 'Silly Jeffrey. I wonder how on earth the writer came up with that?'

'Goodness knows,' said Jeffrey, starting the engine. 'So, do you fancy it? You'd be co-starring with Cassie Craven.'

'Hmm,' said Ellie May. 'That sounds lovely, obviously. I think Cassie is a very talented person and I would completely love to be in a film with her.

One day. Maybe when I'm really old. But there's this other film that I heard about yesterday, and it sounds much more my kind of thing.'

'Really? What is it?' asked Jeffrey.

'It's called *All By Myself*,' said Ellie May, 'and it's about a girl who lives on a desert island for a hundred years. On her own. And no one ever comes to visit. Doesn't that sound fun? You know, the more I think about it, the more I like it! In fact, Jeffrey, I've decided. Yes, my next film is going to be all about ME.'

'I'm not totally sure about the moral of this story, either,' said Jeffrey.

The End

Ellie May's ☆ ☆
☆ New Best Friend!

● ● ● ● ● ● ● ● ● ● ● ● ● ● ● ●

Everyone's talking about this summer's hottest movie, *Ugly Duckling*, so *Giggle* went to chat to its two stars, Ellie May and Fleur. We asked Ellie May what it was like to work alongside such a talented newcomer.

'It's been brilliant,' Ellie May told us. 'I've enjoyed every single moment. We didn't fight at all and anyone who tells you that we did is totally wrong. Me and Fleur are best best friends and I'm hoping that I'll get to do some modelling with her soon. Maybe for a shampoo because I have really nice hair.'

Fleur was also keen to tell us what a great time she'd had. 'I've really enjoyed being in *Ugly Duckling* but, to be honest, I'm looking forward to getting back to modelling. It's a lot easier.'

❝ I'm hoping that I'll get to do some modelling with her soon ❞

We asked whether it was true that Fleur would soon be modelling alongside Ellie May. 'That would be lovely,' said Fleur, 'but my next job is somewhere very far away and top secret, so I don't think so, no.'

Turn to page 46 NOW for twenty top tips to transform YOU from Ugly Duckling to beautiful swan!

Could YOU be a Hollywood stuntman?

Take Giggle's test to find out!

1 Are you afraid of heights?

A. Yes.

B. No.

C. Don't know.

2 Can you drive a car?

A. No.

B. Yes.

C. Sometimes I drive several cars at once.

3 Can you ride a horse?

A. No.

B. Yes.

C. I can ride a horse. And I can speak horse, too.

4 What's your favourite food?
A. Cake.
B. Steak.
C. Snake.

5 Are you nervous of pain?
A. Yes.
B. No.
C. I've heard about pain. What's it like?

6 Would you mind being encased in an enormous block of ice?
A. Yes.
B. No.
C. I already am.

7 What's the most terrifying thing that's ever happened to you?
A. I got stung by a wasp.
B. I stepped on a wasps' nest.
C. I had to prevent the destruction of the universe.

8 You're locked in battle with a giant squid. Who would win?

    A. The squid would.

    B. I would.

    C. I do not fight my own kind.

9 Choose the word you think best describes fire.

    A. Scary!

    B. Exciting!

    C. Friend.

10 Would you like to be a Hollywood stuntman?

    A. No.

    B. Yes.

    C. What's a stuntman?

RESULTS

If you answered mostly A's:

You're probably not very well suited to being a Hollywood stuntman. But don't worry, there are lots of other fun careers out there. You could grow marshmallows, or test out new types of kitten.

If you answered mostly B's:

Congratulations! You should definitely consider a career as a Hollywood stuntman!

If you answered mostly C's:

Return to your planet.
You do not belong here.

EGMONT LUCKY COIN

Our story began over a century ago, when seventeen-year-old Egmont Harald Petersen found a coin in the street.

He was on his way to buy a flyswatter, a small hand-operated printing machine that he then set up in his tiny apartment.

The coin brought him such good luck that today Egmont has offices in over 30 countries around the world. And that lucky coin is still kept at the company's head offices in Denmark.

Marianne Levy

Before she started writing books, Marianne was an actress. Not the incredibly famous sort, though. After graduating from Cambridge University she appeared in a few TV shows and did a bit of comedy on Radio 4. She has been in one film, in which she managed to forget both her lines. Since then, Marianne has written for *The Story of Tracy Beaker*, introduced *America's Next Top Model* and been the voice of a yogurt. She lives in London, and spends her spare time eating cheese and hassling other people's dogs. For news and fun stuff and to see Marianne read an extract from Ellie May, visit **www.mariannelevy.com**

Ali Pye

Ali has always wanted to illustrate books, apart from a short time when she was seven-and-a-half and decided that she'd make a good police-dog handler. Luckily for the Alsations of Great Britain, Ali stuck (sort of) to plan A and eventually achieved her ambition. On the way, Ali studied fashion communication (this was part of the 'sort of'), which is very useful now she's drawing Ellie May's amazing outfits. Ali lives in London with her husband and children. Her favourite things are Arctic foxes, Chinese food and wearing too much eyeliner. You can see some early sketches of Ellie May at Ali's website, **www.alipye.com**

STARRING SOON IN A BOOKSHOP NEAR YOU

ELLIE MAY

Can Definitely be Trusted to Keep a Secret